ISBN 978-1-84135-932-8

Text copyright © Award Publications Limited
Illustrations copyright © Val Biro

This edition published 2012

Published by Award Publications Limited, The Old Riding School,
The Welbeck Estate, Worksop, Nottinghamshire, S80 3LR

14 2

Printed in China

Animal Tales for Bedtime

by Linda Jennings

adapted by

Jackie Andrews and Sophie Giles

Illustrated by Val Biro

Award Publications Limited

The Lonely Goat

There was once a little mountain goat called Jack. He had no brothers and no sisters to play with and was very lonely. So one day he hopped all the way down the mountain to find a friend.

At the bottom he came to a lake. He looked into the water and he saw a little goat exactly like himself.

"Hello," bleated Jack happily. He bent down to touch the other goat's nose, but the water rippled and the little face disappeared.

"Ha, ha," chortled Henry, a mean, grey goat who had

been watching Jack. "How silly! Don't you know you are looking at your own reflection? There's no other goat there at all!"

Poor Jack! He plodded home, feeling sad and foolish.

"I'll never find a friend to play with," he sighed.

The sun was setting when Jack returned to the high pasture where he lived with his mum and dad.

"Jack!" cried his dad. "Where have you been? You've shouldn't give your mother all this worry when she's already got so much on her mind."

"Where is Mum?" asked Jack.

"Come and see," said Dad.

Jack quickly followed. And what a surprise was waiting for him! There was Mother goat and a tiny white kid wobbling beside her on unsteady legs.

"Meet your new little sister!" said Mother goat.

Jack bleated happily. He knew he would never be lonely again.

Ruby's Beautiful Webs

Ruby the spider spins the most beautiful webs. But the problem with cobwebs is that people don't like them and they rush for a duster and sweep them away.

Spring-cleaning time is the very worst time for spiders. Poor Ruby used to scuttle from one house to the next to try to spin a web that wouldn't be swept away.

But one day Ruby happened to find a crooked little cottage that hadn't been spring-cleaned for years.

Now, you might think that such a house would be forgotten and empty, but it's not! It belongs to a rather unusual lady called Grizella. For Grizella is a kindly old witch, and she simply loves to see the beautiful webs Ruby spins each day in the corners and over the shelves.

Ruby couldn't be happier in her new home!

The Pony-Pup

Josh gently patted the tiny puppy that Dad had brought home. It looked almost like a rabbit with its grey fur and floppy ears.

"He's so small!" exclaimed Josh. "I'll call him Titch."

But soon Titch began to grow. At three months old he was the size of a terrier. At four months he was a big as a spaniel. And at six months Titch looked like a labrador with long ears. By the time he was a year old Titch was as big as an Irish wolfhound, which is as big a dog as you will find anywhere. And still he grew.

"Titch seems a silly name for him now," said Dad, as he watched Josh's sister Emily riding on Titch's back.

"He's not a dog, he's a pony," giggled Emily.

"Titch, the pony-pup!" laughed Josh as the three of them trotted around the garden.

Kerry's Kitten

Kerry noticed a little cat on her way home from school one day. It was black, with a little white face, four white paws, and big green eyes.

"Oooh, isn't it sweet!" cried Kerry.

"Best leave it alone," said Kerry's mum. "It probably belongs to the people on the other side of the hedge."

But Kerry thought about the little cat all the way home. She felt sure it wanted to come with her. She kept turning round to look back down the road to see if it was following, but she couldn't see it.

That night it was very warm, and Kerry left her bedroom window open. She went to bed and was soon fast asleep.

When she woke up in the night, Kerry found she couldn't move her feet. Something was sitting on them! She looked down the bed and was not at all surprised to see the little black cat curled up on the duvet.

"I knew you wanted to come and live with me,"
whispered Kerry, stroking the little cat's head. "I'm
going to call you Kitty Smartypants, because you knew
exactly where to find me."

The little cat purred and purred.

Kerry's mother asked all their neighbours if they
knew who had lost a little black cat with a white face,
but no one in the village had heard of a missing kitten.

So Kitty Smartypants lived happily with Kerry and
her mum for many years.

Egg Hunt

Matilda was Farmer Todd's best hen. Sometimes she would lay ten eggs in a week! But Matilda would lay one egg in the barn, one under the hedge, one by the pond, and even one in Farmer Todd's boots! Anywhere but in one of the nice nesting boxes in the hen-house.

"It's no good," complained Farmer Todd. "I don't have all day to go searching for eggs. She'll have to go."

But Amy Todd didn't want Matilda to go. Matilda was her very favourite hen.

The next day, when Amy spotted Matilda hurrying away from the noisy hen-house, she realised exactly what was wrong. "I think I know just what you need, Matilda," whispered Amy.

Amy took an old wooden box from the barn, lined it with straw and placed it in the shade, hidden by the branches of a willow-tree.

Now Matilda Hen goes off to her own special nesting box and lays all her eggs in the secret spot, only she and the Todd family know about. Peace and quiet at last!

The Third Little Pig

Everyone knows the story of the Three Little Pigs, and how one little pig was so clever that he outsmarted the Big Bad Wolf and was safe and sound in his sturdy little house built out of bricks.

The trouble with the third little pig was that he grew terribly smug. Everyone was always telling him how clever he was for outwitting the Big Bad Wolf, and he would strut around, full of his own self-importance.

One day a man came to live next door to the third little pig. He was big and red-faced and drove a van.

"I'm Mr Cleaver," said the man, tipping his hat as he introduced himself. "Pleased to meet you."

"Pleased to meet you, too," said the third little pig. "Of course, you will have heard all about me and how very clever I am."

"Yes indeed," said the red-faced man. "I hear that you are a most intelligent pig."

Very soon the little pig and Mr Cleaver were the best of friends. "You must come to my dinner party tonight," said Mr Cleaver one day. "You'll have pride of place on the table – I mean, *at* the table."

"I'd be delighted," said the little pig, feeling even more pleased with himself than usual.

Later that day, as the third little pig was getting ready for the dinner party there was a *rat-tat-tat* at the door. It was Danny Dog. "You'll have to be quick because I've been invited out to dinner," the little pig explained.

"That's just it," yelped Danny Dog. "You must not go!"

"Why ever not?" asked the third little pig, crossing his arms. "You're only jealous because you haven't been invited as well."

"But you've been invited *for* dinner, not *to* dinner!" cried Danny. "I was trotting down the high street, and I saw Mr Cleaver's van parked outside his shop – the butcher's shop! Mr Cleaver is a butcher!"

"Oh dear," gasped the third little pig, and he began to tremble.

As fast as he could, the third little pig packed his bags and off he went to build another brick house far away from Mr Cleaver.

And he stopped boasting about how he had outwitted the Big Bad Wolf. The third little pig realised that he wasn't quite so clever after all!

Motorway Dog

When he was a puppy, Pip had been loved by everyone. But now he was grown up the children didn't play with him as much and their father grumbled about Pip's enormous appetite.

"That dog just has to go," the father muttered to himself one day.

Pip overheard this and so that night, after the family had gone to bed, he crept out of his kennel, took a last look at the house, hung his head sadly and set off down the lane.

He walked and walked. The lane became a road, and the road became a motorway. Pip was frightened by all the noise. He didn't know where he was, and he was very tired. He squeezed through the hedge and into a field to hide from the traffic, and soon fell asleep.

He woke up, trembling. On the other side of the hedge hundreds of cars and lorries thundered past in clouds of smelly fumes. And standing over him he saw a big brown bull!

"What are you doing in my field?" snorted the bull.

"I'm sorry! I'm lost," stammered Pip. It seemed that nobody wanted him around.

Just then, a car pulled in to the lay-by and a family got out. "There's a nice field for our picnic," said a small voice. Pip drooled at the thought of a tasty picnic. Sausage rolls! Ham sandwiches! Chicken legs!

Whining softly, he padded up to the family.

"Look, Dad, a dog. He looks awfully hungry."

"And he hasn't got a collar," said Dad, patting Pip.

"I bet some awful person left him here," cried the boy.

The children's mother held out a sausage and Pip gently took it. In two bites it was gone! Gratefully he wagged his tail.

"We can't leave him here," said Mum, "not with that motorway so near. It's much too dangerous."

So when the family packed up their picnic, they took Pip with them. The boy opened the car door, and Pip sprang in and settled down thankfully on the floor.

"Home we all go!" said Dad, and Pip sighed a big happy sigh.

The Chatterbox

Mrs Peasbody was a terrible chatterbox. She talked morning, noon and night. Even when her husband pretended to be asleep, Mrs Peasbody would chatter on.

One day Farmer Griffiths came to her door.

"Oh, Farmer Griffiths," Mrs Peasbody began. "Fancy seeing you. I was just saying to George that the last time we saw you—"

Farmer Griffiths interrupted her, for he knew he wouldn't get a word in edgewise if he didn't.

"Mrs Peasbody," he said, "I was wondering if I could please rent your field for my donkey."

"Of course you can," said Mrs Peasbody. "Do you know—" But Farmer Griffiths had already turned around and left to fetch his donkey.

The next morning Mrs Peasbody went to see the little donkey in the field at the bottom of the garden. She leaned on the wall and she talked and talked and talked!

Hours later, Mrs Peasbody was still talking and the little donkey began to nod his head at the sound of her voice going on and on and on.

Suddenly the donkey fell over. "Oh my!" cried Mrs Peasbody. "I'd better get Farmer Griffiths at once."

"Where have his back legs gone?" he cried when he saw the donkey lying on its back, and he called the vet.

"Hmm. No legs…" said the vet, looking puzzled.

"They were here this morning," said Mrs Peasbody.

"It's very rare indeed," said the vet, "but have you ever heard of people talking the hind legs off a donkey?"

"Is it curable?" asked Farmer Griffiths anxiously.

"Your donkey needs plenty of rest and no noise," prescribed the vet, putting some earplugs into the donkey's long, floppy ears.

Mrs Peasbody was so upset that she didn't speak to anyone for a whole week!

But the little donkey's legs soon grew back again as good as new, and from then on he was always careful to stay away from Mrs Peasbody, just in case!

19

The Big Fright

A family of frogs once lived in a beautiful garden pond. It had green wavy weeds, waterlilies, and a little stone statue pouring water from an urn. Around the edges there were flat stones and flowering plants.

One day the owners of the garden came and put something new in the pond. The frogs hid amongst the waterlilies until the people had gone, then one bold little frog popped out of the water to take a look.

Quickly he dived down again, shaking with fright.

"There's a big horrible bird up there," he cried, "with a wicked-looking beak and long spindly legs."

"That sounds like a heron," said an old frog. "And herons eat frogs."

The frogs hid under the water and croaked forlornly.

But the bold little frog could not resist having another peek at the new arrival. "It's still there," he told the others. "It hasn't moved an inch."

"No," said the old frog. "Herons stay very still until a frog swims near them, then – *swish! crunch!* – that's the end of the frog."

The bold little frog was very upset.

"He'll spoil all our fun!" he thought to himself. "I'm going to try to give that heron such a fright, he'll go away for good!"

And he swam up behind the bird and leaped straight up onto its back!

But he didn't land on soft warm feathers. Oh, no. Instead he slipped and slid all the way down the heron's back and splashed right into the pond.

"It's not a real bird at all," he told the other frogs. "It's a statue made of metal!"

The frogs swam to the surface to see for themselves, and soon they were leaping and splashing all over the metal heron.

Far from spoiling the frogs' fun, the heron was the best plaything they had ever had!

The Dancing Bear

Bobo was a dancing bear and he travelled through towns and villages, dancing to the music his master Frederick played. But even though Frederick was kind to him, Bobo was not always happy.

Bobo remembered when he was a tiny bear cub, living in a big forest with a green meadow running down to a swift-flowing river. He remembered how he had loved playing in the forest with the other cubs.

But hunters had trapped Bobo in a big net and took him away to market and he never saw his family again.

Not knowing Bobo had been stolen from his mother, Frederick had bought him and taught him to dance.

One day Frederick and Bobo arrived at a little town on top of a hill. There was a fair in the meadow below the castle, and Bobo and his master made their way towards it.

The meadow sloped all the way down to a rushing river, and beyond that lay a forest. As soon as Bobo saw it, something stirred in him.

Could it be his old home?

Frederick saw how Bobo gazed sadly at the forest and he suddenly felt very sorry for him. He stopped playing his flute and untied the chain around Bobo's neck.

"Go on, old friend. It's time for you to go home."

Bobo hugged Frederick, then ran down the grassy bank towards the river. Before he vanished into the forest, Bobo turned and there on the hill was Frederick smiling and waving goodbye.

Rescuing Rosie

One day on a visit to the park, Gemma found a little duckling waddling alone. It quacked sadly and looked lost. "You poor thing," said Gemma. She looked all around the pond, but she couldn't find its mother. So she took the duckling home with her and called it Rosie.

Mum made a cosy bed for the duckling from a shoebox filled with pillow feathers. She put the box on the draining board, and filled the sink with water. Now Rosie had a warm nest and a pond all of her own!

The little duckling followed Gemma everywhere. And when Gemma went to school, Rosie would creep into her shoebox nest and quack sadly until she returned.

But one morning, when Gemma arrived at school her friends were laughing and pointing. Gemma turned around.

"Rosie!" she gasped in surprise. She was secretly
delighted that the duckling had followed her!

It was too late to take Rosie home, so Gemma took
her into the classroom. The little duckling sat happily
on Gemma's lap all day.

In no time, Rosie had grown up, and Mum said
Gemma should really take her back to the pond, where
she belonged.

"She'll never leave me," thought Gemma.

But when they reached the pond a handsome-looking
drake waddled up to them and fluffed up his feathers,
and Rosie hopped into the water and swam across the
pond with her new friend. Gemma waved goodbye and
walked sadly home.

A few months later Gemma opened the back door to
find Rosie outside – now a proud mother duck with
seven little ducklings.

"I'm just visiting," she seemed to say as she
quack-quacked, and off she waddled down the
path, her little family following behind.

The Lazy Squirrel

It was the most beautiful autumn any of the animals in Leafy Wood could remember. The days were so warm it was tempting to sit around basking in the sun. But as every squirrel knew, there was work to be done. The wood was a hive of activity as all the squirrels busily collected nuts for the long winter.

All the squirrels, that is, except for Dudley.

"There's still plenty of time later to gather nuts for my winter store," he said as he napped in a sunny glade.

The other squirrels shook their heads disapprovingly.

"What a lazy young squirrel," they said.

Before long, the weather turned cold.

The days soon grew shorter, and grey clouds seemed to forever cover the sky. Strong winds blew all the leaves from the trees as the branches swayed back and forth.

"I won't even have to pull the nuts from the branches. They will fall down in the wind," said lazy Dudley.

But, to his dismay, there were no nuts to be found anywhere. "If only I hadn't been so lazy!" he thought as he crept home, sad and hungry.

Fortunately, the other squirrels took pity on him and shared any spare nuts they had with him.

It was a long winter, and Dudley learned an important lesson. When spring came at last, he was the first to be up and about, eager to help his friends build their dreys and gather food. Dudley was never lazy again!

Nesting Time

It was the first day of spring and Mr and Mrs Robin were house-hunting. Mrs Robin wanted a bigger nest in which to lay her eggs, but was very choosy.

"The scarecrow's pockets will be too small once our chicks are here!" she chirped to Mr Robin.

Mr Robin flew everywhere trying to find a tree for their new nest. But all the trees he showed to Mrs Robin were too tall, or too short, or too shady. Then, just as he was about to give up, he found the perfect home inside the shed at the bottom of the garden.

It was a big silver box with a window in the front. There was plenty of room inside it for a nest.

One day after the chicks had hatched the shed door opened and a man came in. "Come quick, Laura!" he cried. "There's a robin's nest inside the old television."

The man's wife came to the shed and looked in. "How lovely!" she said. "We've got a real live nature show!"

Caspar's Hump

Caspar Camel was fed up with life at the zoo and giving rides to children. He grumbled to himself as his keeper, Jenny, led him down the path to the waiting visitors.

"You're in a bad mood today, Caspar!" said Jenny.

"He's got the hump!" giggled the children.

"Right," thought Caspar. "No one is having rides!"

He refused to kneel down to let the children get onto his back. "What a pity," said Jenny, "because I was going to send Caspar to the new safari park. He'd like it there, but they won't want a grumpy camel!"

At the mention of moving to a safari park, Caspar forgot his glum mood quick as a flash. He knelt down and nudged a child onto his back for a ride.

"I see you've lost your hump, Caspar," smiled Jenny.

"But he's still got two on his back," laughed a child.

This time everybody giggled – even Caspar.

29

Going Like the Wind

Lion couldn't wait to tell the other animals his brilliant idea. "Let's run a race," he said, "and the winner will have their food gathered by everyone else for a week!"

Tortoise didn't like the sound of Lion's idea at all.

"The small and slow animals can start further along the track, so it is as fair as it can be," suggested Lion.

Even so, everyone knew that Cheetah would win, because he was the fastest animal in the world.

Lion made everyone line up to start the race. Cheetah had to go right at the back, behind all the other animals.

"Ready, set, GO!" roared Lion, and the race began.

Mrs Lion waited at the finishing post to see who would get there first. She didn't know why she should bother, though, since Cheetah was bound to win.

She gave a yawn and as she did there was a sudden gust of wind and the ground shook.

"What on earth was *that*?" she wondered.

Soon after, little Antelope came springing past the finishing post and Mrs Lion declared her the winner.

Antelope was delighted that she wouldn't have to search for food for a whole week!

But where was Cheetah? Had he got lost? Nobody had seen him since the start of the race.

That night, as the animals celebrated Antelope's win, from out of the darkness Cheetah appeared, looking very tired. He explained that he had been running so fast that he had overshot the finishing post. He had only stopped when he finally splashed into a watering hole!

"So it *was* Cheetah who won the race," said Mrs Lion, remembering the gust of wind and the shaking earth.

But Cheetah didn't want to take the prize away from Antelope.

"Speed is no good unless you can put the brakes on!" he declared. And everyone agreed.

The Long and the Tall

William was a great big Irish wolfhound, and Danny was a dachshund. They were great friends: they shared the same basket and even the same food bowl. But when it came to going for a walk together, they had a problem.

William could run like the wind, but for every stride he took, poor little Danny had to sprint ten paces. Danny could play with the small dogs, but he just couldn't keep up with his friend.

Whilst William could see right across the park to the wood, with its deer and rabbits, and a wide lake that was lovely and cool to swim in, poor little Danny couldn't see any of these wonderful things.

He was always tired out before he'd gone even halfway across the park. So William would go off by himself, leaving Danny to sniff around the bushes or play with the other small dogs like him.

One day, when Danny chased a ball into the shrubbery he found something that made him very excited. It was a skateboard!

Danny had often seen the children riding skateboards, and he knew they could go very fast.

It gave him an idea.

When William came back from his long walk, he helped Danny push the skateboard all the way home with his nose.

The next morning they attached a piece of string to one end of it, and then Danny climbed aboard.

William took the other end of the string in his mouth and pulled little Danny down the path, across the road, and all the way to the park – then right across to the far side where he'd never been before.

It was wonderful!

William showed Danny all his favourite places in the wood, and together they chased rabbits in and out of the trees for fun and paddled in the shallow water at the edge of the lake.

From that day on William and Danny went everywhere together, no matter how far it was!

Sebastian Fox

Sebastian Fox felt sorry for himself. He had often heard the stories people tell about Big Bad Foxes who stole chickens and gobbled them up for their supper. "I'm not like that," said Sebastian. "I'm a nice, friendly fox."

He decided he would try to prove it.

First he went to Farmer Baxter's chicken run. He looked through the wire and smiled at the silly chickens who were all huddled in a corner, squawking loudly.

"Hello," said Sebastian. "I'm a friendly fox!"

"That's what they all say," said the cockerel. "Then we let you in and you eat us! Go away!"

Suddenly there was a shout and Farmer Baxter came running from the farmhouse, waving a big stick.

"Get away!" cried Farmer Baxter. "Shoo!"

Poor Sebastian scampered away through the woods.

He paused to catch his breath and a family of woodpeckers squawked and flapped away from him.

"I only want to make friends," sniffed Sebastian. "I'm a friendly fox." But it seemed that nobody liked him.

Sebastian felt terribly sad and lonely. Nobody wanted to be his friend.

He was creeping back to his den when a group of schoolchildren walked past.

"Look, Miss, it's a fox," one of them cried. "Isn't he beautiful!"

"Careful, children, don't scare him," said the teacher. "Yes, you can take a picture, Imogen. We'll put it up on the wall for Open Day."

Sebastian stood still with his head held high and his fine bushy tail fluffed out.

Snap! went the camera, and the children walked on, chattering excitedly about the handsome fox.

Sebastian smiled happily. His photo would go up on the classroom wall! Someone did like him after all.

The Troublesome Rhinoceros

There was once a group of jungle animals who were all great friends. "It's too hot here in the jungle for us to be falling out with each other," said Lion. "We should take things easy." And everyone agreed.

One very hot day an enormous rhinoceros came thundering through the trees. He had a long horn on the end of his nose and he looked very fierce!

"Can we help you?" asked Lion politely.

"I'm Rhino and I've come to live with you," roared the rhinoceros.

"And what do you do best?" asked Lion. "For every animal who joins our group has a particular skill."

"I can stampede," said Rhino in a gruff voice. "And I can trample bushes and spike things with my horn."

"But we live in peace. We don't want anyone being troublesome here."

"But that's boring!" roared Rhino, and he charged off again into the trees.

Suddenly the animals heard a loud *SCRUNCH*!

Monkey swung off through the trees to see what had happened and soon she was back, chuckling merrily.

"Come and see," she said to the other animals.

Monkey led them to an enormous tree. There was Rhino, with his horn stuck fast in the trunk.

"Will somebody help me?" he asked in a small voice.

"Only if you promise never to stampede through the jungle again," said Elephant.

Rhino promised, and Elephant curled his long trunk around the rhinoceros's middle and pulled him free.

After that, Rhino was as good as his word.

He came to live with the friendly animals. And he only ever used his horn to spear fruit for the monkeys and parrots.

Fancy Dress

The animals of Oakapple Wood were very excited when Max Mouse read out the notice on the big oak tree. "Delilah Duck is having a fancy dress party," he cried. Everyone chattered with delight.

"I'm going as Mickey Mouse – that's easy!" said Max.

"And I'll be Peter Rabbit," said Rory Rabbit.

"And I'll dress up as a clown," added Billy Badger.

Harriet Hedgehog crept sadly away, unnoticed by the excited crowd that had gathered to discuss the party. She looked at herself in the pond in Farmer Baxter's field, and a tear rolled down her cheek.

"I can't dress up as anything," she sobbed. "My sharp prickles will stick through any material. I'd look silly."

Harriet shuffled off through the grass, until she came to Farmer Baxter's garden where the children were having a party.

Harriet could see all kinds of delicious snacks laid out on the table under the apple tree. There were sausage rolls and crisps, cakes and sandwiches, and… What was *that*? It looked just like a hedgehog!

But taking a closer look, Harriet saw that it was really half a grapefruit covered with little sticks. On the end of each stick was a tiny piece of cheese.

This gave her an idea for a fancy dress costume.

Harriet was the last to arrive at Delilah Duck's party, and it was already growing dark. She smiled to herself as she shuffled slowly along the moonlit path.

As she drew near she could hear the other animals laughing and giggling to each other as they admired each other's costumes.

But then an extraordinary sight met their eyes. Coming along the path like a clockwork toy was a very strange-looking creature indeed.

It was Harriet Hedgehog! And stuck all over her prickles were lots and lots of acorns.

"I'm a party treat for squirrels!" she announced with a smile. "They can pull acorns from my prickles to eat!"

All the animals thought it such an original – and tasty – outfit that they gave her first prize in the fancy dress competition!

The Wrong Pole

It was the first day of the school holidays and Ben had planned to go on a bike ride with his best friend, Jake. He'd been looking forward to it for ages, but it was raining outside, and Dad said it was too wet to go.

So instead Ben got out his colouring pencils and some paper and spread them out on the kitchen table.

He drew a snowy scene with a polar bear and lots of penguins sitting on ice floes. It had lots of detail and Ben was really enjoying himself.

"Polar bears live in the North Pole; penguins live at the South Pole," Ben's older brother chuckled. "Everyone knows you never see them together, silly!"

Ben felt foolish. He had worked hard all morning and he loved his picture. So he scooped up his colouring pencils and ran to his room, where he pinned his picture on the wall.

That night Ben had a strange dream.

He was sitting on an ice floe next to a penguin when he heard an unhappy growly voice. "Will you help me? I'm lost and I want to go home."

It was Ben's polar bear!

Ben knew it was his fault the polar bear was stuck at the wrong pole.

The next morning when he woke up, Ben knew exactly what he had to do.

Before anyone else was awake, Ben carefully painted out the polar bear and drew a penguin in his place. Then he took another sheet of paper and drew another snowy scene. But this time he drew lots and lots of polar bears! One of them was smiling, as if to say 'thank you'!

That day it was sunny at last and Ben and Jake went on their bike ride.

"Where shall we cycle to?" asked Jake.

"The North Pole!" laughed Ben as the pair of them set out for a day of adventure.

Fred the Racing Donkey

Fred the donkey lived in a meadow,
where children came to feed him carrots.
In the next field were some racehorses who teased Fred
when he tried to keep up as they galloped about.

"You can't keep up with us!" they'd laugh. And they
would boast about the famous races they had won. One
horse, called Black Prince, had even won the Derby!

"I wish I could win a race," sighed Fred.

That afternoon the farmer's daughter, Beth, came to
feed Fred. "We've got a surprise for you," she smiled,
and she led him to the field at the bottom of the lane.

It was filled with people and lots of donkeys!

"It's the Donkey Derby – a special race just for donkeys,"
said Beth. "My brother Sam is going to ride you!"

Fred only knew about the horse-race called the Derby.
Black Prince never stopped boasting about winning it.

He'd show those horses. He'd win the Donkey Derby!

A whistle blew and the race began! Fred imagined himself to be a big racehorse and galloped as fast as he could. He passed one rider after another, until there was only one donkey left in front of him.

The race commentator was very excited. "Here comes Fred, coming up on the outside! … Conker and Fred are neck-and-neck as they come up to the finishing post! … And it's Fred! Fred wins the Donkey Derby!"

That evening Fred proudly wore his winner's rosette.

"What's that?" called one of the racehorses.

"I won a race today!" Fred grinned.

"I bet it's a race no one has ever heard of," sneered Black Prince.

"It's the Derby," said Fred. "I won the Derby!"

The horses were astonished. From that day on they never again teased Fred for being a slow little donkey!

Tim Tiger

Tim Tiger wanted to be just like his famous uncle who was always appearing in nature shows on television.

"When's your uncle coming to visit?" asked an excited tiger cub.

"Oh, I don't know," sighed Tim. "He's always so very busy." And he padded off into the bushes to sulk. Life in the safari park was so boring, thought Tim. It would be much more exciting to be famous.

One day Tim was snoozing under a tree when he felt his whiskers twitch and he heard a giggle. Opening his eyes he saw a little boy sitting in front of him.

Tim Tiger was such a big softie that he gently picked up the boy in his mouth and trotted out from the trees to find his parents.

"He's got our baby! He's going to eat our baby!" shrieked the boy's mother, waving her arms in panic.

Tim carefully set the boy down on the grass and gently patted him on the head with his huge paw. The little boy threw his arms around Tim's neck.

The woman burst into noisy tears. "Oh my goodness! The tiger has rescued my little boy!" she sobbed.

After that, news spread, and hundreds of people came to the safari park to see Tim Tiger. Everyone wanted to have their photo taken with him. He was famous at last!

But Tim soon began to tire of all the excitement and longed for a quiet life, sleeping under the trees. "Being famous isn't all it's cracked up to be!" he says.

45

The Magician's Rabbit

Ronnie was a magician's rabbit. He knew just how to hide at the right moment so that when Mr Alfonso pulled him out of the hat, it looked like magic.

"It's just a trick, though," thought Ronnie. "I wish I could really be a magic rabbit."

One day Ronnie was out on the lawn nibbling grass when a witch flew by. Now was his chance!

"Excuse me, madam!" he called. "Can you help me?"

The witch smiled. "Why, you're the magician's rabbit, aren't you?" she said.

"But I'm not *really* magic," said Ronnie, "and everyone knows it. I wish I were really magical."

"Do you, now? In that case, I think I can help you." And the witch muttered some magic words.

That evening at a children's party, Ronnie sprang out of the magician's hat as usual.

"Everyone knows that old trick. That's not proper magic!" called out a rude little boy.

But just as the little boy spoke, Ronnie started to grow larger and larger and larger!

"Help! It's a monster rabbit!" cried the boy, and all the children rushed to the door. Poor Mr Alfonso was horrified. No one would hire him for parties now!

But just as the children reached the door, Ronnie began to shrink again. In seconds he was back to his normal size and the children tiptoed back into the room.

"Are you sure you know how that 'old trick' is done?" Ronnie chuckled as the little boy stood staring, mouth wide open.

"Wow!" gasped the children. "A talking rabbit! That *is* real magic!"

Panda Friends

Polly Panda was the children's favourite animal at the zoo. There aren't many giant pandas like her left in the world, and certainly Polly was the only one in the zoo.

"Wouldn't you like a panda friend, Polly?" the children asked.

But Polly didn't want a friend. She didn't want to share her bamboo shoots, and her little cosy house – and she worried that she wouldn't be the children's favourite any more.

One day Polly's keeper gave her a big, cheerful smile. "I have a surprise for you, Polly," he said. "Can you guess what it is?"

But Polly didn't need to guess. She knew what it would be – another panda!

Someone else to eat her bamboo shoots. Someone else to sleep in her little house. Someone else for the children to make a fuss of.

The next day the new panda arrived. His name was Boris. "You have a beautiful place here, Polly," said Boris as he looked around his new home.

But Polly turned her back on him and chewed sulkily on her bamboo shoots, without offering to share them.

"Ooh, look!" cried the children. "Polly's sulking!"

Polly knew she was being unfriendly, but she couldn't help herself. Boris gazed sadly at Polly, not knowing what else to do.

And so it went on. Boris was too polite to take his share of the bamboo shoots. He let Polly eat them all.

Poor Boris became thinner and thinner, while Polly grew fatter and fatter.

The children stopped talking to Polly because of her nasty behaviour and she began to feel very lonely.

One day, as Boris slept, Polly touched his nose to wake him. "I'm sorry," she said. "I've been a selfish panda."

Being the good fellow he was, Boris forgave her and the two of them now live happily together. And Polly loves having a friend to play with when all the children have gone home.

Flopsy's Garden

Flopsy was a beautiful lop-eared rabbit with soft black fur. He lived in a hutch in a big, wild garden and every day he was let out so that he could hop about the lawn.

One day Flopsy spotted some strange rabbits at the bottom of the garden. "They do look odd!" thought Flopsy. "They're brown, and their ears stick right up."

"What are you?" asked one rabbit, staring at Flopsy.

"I'm a rabbit," said Flopsy. "Just like you."

"You can't be!" snapped an older rabbit. "Rabbits are brown and they have sticking up ears like this."

"You must be some sort of strange pet – a ferret or something like that!" jeered a big rabbit as he thumped his back feet in warning.

Poor Flopsy! He turned and fled back to his hutch.

Just then a pretty little wild rabbit popped out of a bush. "Well, I *like* your droopy ears and your black fur," she said.

Every day after that, Flopsy played hide-and-seek with his new friend. And in time, the brown rabbits all came to the garden to join in. Very soon they forgot about their differences. A rabbit is a rabbit, after all.

Henry's Day Out

Henry Hamster lived in a cage in Mia Brown's house, where he looked out at the garden, daydreaming of exciting outdoor adventures as he ran in his wheel.

Then one day Mia left Henry's cage door open. Seeing his chance, Henry scurried across the floor and out of the kitchen door. He was in the garden!

But outside the house everything looked so big. Even the pond seemed like an ocean to the little hamster.

Henry twitched his little nose and smelt the sweet flowers. Then he smelt something that made his fur stand on end. It was Tabitha, Mia's cat!

Henry stood as still as a stone. But Tabitha was not fooled. *Wham!* A big furry paw pinned poor Henry to the ground. At that moment Mia came into the garden.

"Tabitha, what have you got there? Let go at once!" Tabitha released Henry and sped off across the lawn.

"How did you get out here?" Mia wondered as she carried Henry back inside. And as he climbed into his wheel, Henry decided he liked it better indoors after all!

Wanda Witch's New Kitten

One day Boppo the wizard went to visit his old friend, Wanda Witch, and he brought her a present: a cute, fluffy ginger kitten.

Now Wanda was far too polite to say so, but as adorable as he was, she didn't really want the little ginger kitten.

It was true that she needed a new cat, since her last one had gone to live wild in the forest – but a *ginger* kitten! Everyone knew that a witch's cat had to be black.

She would be the laughing-stock of all the other witches.

But the ginger kitten followed Wanda into the kitchen and wound himself round her legs, purring loudly. Grudgingly, Wanda put down a bowl of food and the kitten ate up every scrap.

Wanda then fetched a paintbrush and a large tin of black fur dye. She had made up her mind she would try to dye the kitten black to be a proper witch's cat.

But the ginger kitten didn't like being painted with the horrible black stuff one little bit. He ran off out of the door and hid under a bush at the end of the garden. Nothing would make him come out, not even a saucer of cream.

Wanda Witch called and called in vain for the kitten to come back, but finally she had to go to bed.

As she pulled up the covers, she thought how nice it was to have a cat again. She wished the kitten would come in and curl up beside her, and keep her company.

That night it rained heavily. "Poor little kitten," thought Wanda. "He'll get so cold and wet out there."

And so it happened that in the middle of the night a smudgy-looking kitten, with its wet fur all standing up in spikes, jumped onto Wanda's bed.

Wanda gently rubbed the kitten dry with a towel, cleaning away the rest of the dye.

"I don't really mind a ginger kitten, after all," she said. "Perhaps I can start a new fashion for witches!"

Nosy Gerald Giraffe

Gerald was a very nosy giraffe. His long neck enabled him to bend his head to hear everything that was going on in the zoo.

Of course, he couldn't help having such a long neck – and seeing what everyone was up to – but he could help being a terrible gossip. Unfortunately, he just couldn't keep anything to himself. Nothing was ever a secret with Gerald around.

"I wish Gerald would hold his tongue," complained Percy the polar bear. "He won't make many friends gossiping the way he does."

Now, one day Gerald heard a commotion in the Parrot House. He wanted to find out what it was all about, and he had to stretch his long neck as far as it would go, and then tilt his head to the side to hear what was going on.

In fact, it wasn't very interesting after all: parrots are noisy birds at the best of times, and they were only squawking to each other about the weather.

Disappointed that he hadn't heard any new secrets, Gerald pulled his neck back again but, to his dismay, he found he had accidentally tied a knot in it!

Poor Gerald! He felt very, very uncomfortable, and no matter what he did, he couldn't untie himself.

The news about Gerald's knotted neck quickly spread around the zoo. The other animals all laughed at him. He looked so funny!

"It serves you right!" they said. "Perhaps that will teach you not to be so nosy!"

Eventually, the zoo vet came and untied Gerald's neck, and it was soon as good as new again.

But Gerald had learned his lesson. He didn't stretch his neck out to hear private conversations any more. And if by chance he did happen to hear anything interesting, he certainly never gossiped about it.

Pony for Sale

Hazelnut was a small brown pony with a black tail and mane. For years she and Martha had been the best of friends but now Martha was too big to ride her.

Martha put her arms round Hazelnut's neck. "We can't keep two ponies, and I need a pony I can ride. I have to sell you." Hazelnut didn't understand, but she knew something was wrong because Martha looked sad.

Soon lots of people began visiting the field. "What's happening?" Hazelnut wondered.

There was a little boy who came to see her. He gave her sugar lumps and whispered in her ear, and he rode her carefully and gently around the field.

But the boy's mother shook her head. "I'm sorry, Jacob, but we really can't afford her," she said sadly.

Soon after, another child came to look at Hazelnut. Instead of asking to ride her, the girl just jumped up and down and cried, "Daddy! I want her!"

Her father looked at Hazelnut and stroked his chin in thought. But Annabel shrieked and stamped her foot.

"You said I could have a pony, Daddy! You *said*!"

"Very well," sighed Annabel's father, "we'll buy her."

And so Hazelnut was off to a new home.

She was led to a clean stable, with a bowl of oats and fresh water. She should have been happy, but she wasn't.

As Hazelnut had guessed, Annabel was very spoilt and treated her badly. When Hazelnut hesitated before a jump, Annabel would dig her hard in the ribs with her heels and tug sharply on the reins.

When Annabel's mother saw this she came running over. "Stop it! Hazelnut will have to go back," she said.

And so Hazelnut found herself back in Martha's paddock. But it wasn't long before the nice little boy, Jacob, came back with his mother. This time he was clutching his piggy bank.

"I've saved up all my pocket money!" smiled Jacob hopefully. "Mum says we can almost meet your price."

"That's okay," said Martha. "I'd just like Hazelnut to go to a good home," she smiled.

The Talent Contest

One day, the jungle animals decided to hold a talent contest. The winner would be the animal whose talent everyone agreed was the most useful.

First came Monkey. "I can swing by my tail and juggle coconuts at the same time," he said.

"That's clever, but it doesn't sound very useful to me," said Zebra. So Monkey was out of the competition.

"I can squirt a jet of water high over the trees," announced Elephant. And to prove it, he did. But he soaked everyone, and so Elephant was disqualified.

"I can sing beautifully," squawked Parrot. But he was terribly out of tune and everyone had to cover their ears.

Tiger was ruled out, too. His only talents seemed to be sleeping and hunting the other animals. And the animals all agreed that none of them liked to be hunted!

Crocodile was next. "I can pretend to be a log floating in the river," he smiled shyly.

But no one was sure that this was very useful either.

Suddenly there was a rumble of thunder and rain began to fall in torrents. All the animals ran for shelter, and soon the river washed away the log bridge.

"Whatever shall I do?" cried Porcupine. "My children are all at school on the other side of the river. I can't get across to bring them home."

"You can walk across on my back," said Crocodile.

"Can I come, too?" squeaked a little mouse.

Soon half a dozen small creatures had climbed on to Crocodile's back and they all safely crossed the river.

"Well, I think we've found the winner of the contest," said Elephant, and the others all agreed. Crocodile certainly had the most useful talent.

Max the Circus Lion

Max was a circus lion. He looked very big and fierce, but really he was a softie and didn't want to eat anyone. The crowds all loved his act with Tyler the lion tamer, and Max was happy. But sometimes he wished he didn't have to live in a cage and travel around the country.

One day his chance came when Tyler left the latch on Max's cage unlocked! The clever lion was able to open it with his teeth and crawl under a caravan, where he waited until there was nobody about. Then, with a great leap, he was off and into the woods beyond.

Max could smell something tasty and he followed the scent through the trees. He poked his head through a leafy bush, sniffing the tantalising smell when…

"Aargh! Help! Help! It's a lion!"

A family, who had just been tucking in to a picnic, leapt to their feet in fright.

"Shoo!" cried Dad, waving a stick at Max.

And they ran away shouting for help.

Max gobbled up the picnic and lay down to sleep. He was happily snoozing in the warm sun when he heard a familiar voice.

"Max! What *are* you doing?" It was Tyler the lion tamer. "You wanted a bit of freedom, didn't you? Well, I've got some good news for you, Max," Tyler continued. "You and I are going to live at a safari park."

Max soon got used to living in the beautiful park where he could roam freely every day. And sometimes Max and Tyler would perform their old circus tricks – just to see the surprise on the visitors' faces!

A Bump in the Night

The holiday cottage stood on a hill overlooking the sea. It was very peaceful. This was Tom's first holiday away from home and he was so excited about all the adventures they had planned.

Mum and Dad had let him stay up later than usual, and when he went to bed he could see the full moon rising over the sea. With a happy sigh and the thought of days swimming in the sea and paddling in rockpools, Tom fell asleep.

Bump! What was that? Tom woke very suddenly with a thumping heart. Someone was making a noise by the back door of the cottage.

"Burglars!" gasped Tom and he crept out of bed and tip-toed across the creaky boards to his parents' room.

"Mum! Dad!" he hissed. "Wake up! There are burglars outside!"

"What!" exclaimed Dad as he leapt out of bed. He followed Tom across to the window where they could hear the rustling and clanging noises outside in the yard. One of the dustbins was being rolled on its side.

"Stay here, Tom," said Dad, as he went downstairs to investigate.

Tom peered out into the darkness. Something shadowy was moving around under the hedge. The dustbin continued to clatter about. Tom stood rigid with fright, but before he knew it, Dad was back beside him.

"Look carefully, Tom, and don't make a sound. You'll see your 'burglars' in a moment." Dad whispered, pointing out of the window.

The moon came out from behind a cloud and flooded the back yard, and Tom saw…

"A badger, Dad! Look! There are two of them!"

"They were raiding the dustbin," laughed Dad. "I expect they liked our left-over beefburgers."

Tom and his mum and dad watched the badgers for a long time. After that they came every night and Mum put out food for them. But Dad tied the dustbin lid shut. Those 'burglars' could make a terrible mess otherwise!

The Big Outdoor Adventure

Molly and Matt Mouse lived in the attic of a big old house. It was a wonderful place for mice, with lots of boxes to gnaw on and – best of all –no humans!

Each night they left the attic to visit Harry's bedroom to eat up the biscuit crumbs he left on the floor.

But one night, instead of biscuit crumbs, they found an enormous piece of cheese stuck on a block of wood.

"Ooh!" cried Molly greedily, and she ran towards it.

But Matt caught hold of her tail. "Stop! It's a trap!"

As the two mice crept back to the attic they saw many more mouse traps laid all over the house.

Things got worse when Harry's dad came up into the attic the next day. "So this is where they're living," he said. "Well, a cat will soon get rid of any mice in here."

In the darkest corner of the attic, the mice trembled in fear. "We'll have to go and live with cousin Meg in the garden," quivered Molly.

So that night the mice scurried downstairs, squeezed under the back door and ran out into the garden.

As they crossed the moonlit lawn a terrifying shadow passed over them, screeching, "Too-whit-too-whoo!"

The two mice quickly scampered into the hedge, and hid trembling under a large leaf. "Oh my! The garden is even more dangerous than the house!" cried Molly.

"We'll have to make a run for it!" said Matt boldly. "It's not far to the garden shed where cousin Meg lives, but we must be quick!"

The mice ran from bush to bush, hiding from the owl.

"We're nearly there!" gasped Molly.

Finally they reached the old ivy-covered shed. And there was cousin Meg, waiting to greet them. They rushed inside, safe at last.

The shed was full of junk. It didn't look like somewhere humans – or cats – visited at all. It was the perfect place for mice to live in peace and quiet!

Sheldon Tortoise's Special Patch

Sheldon Tortoise was very, very old. He had lived in the same garden long before the children were born and he had his own favourite patch behind the garden shed where the wild strawberries grew.

One spring day, after Sheldon awoke from his long winter's sleep, he trundled slowly and happily towards his special patch.

But it was gone! Where the wild strawberries had once grown there was now a ghastly stone patio with little plants growing between the cracks in the stones. Sheldon Tortoise nibbled one of them. "Ugh!" It tasted horrible. The old shed had gone, too. Sheldon did not like change and he began to sulk. He pulled his head back into his shell and hoped everything would be exactly as it used to be when he came back out again.

When Hannah and Alex came out into the garden to say hello, Sheldon ignored them and stayed inside his shell. Even when they put tasty lettuce leaves in front of him he still wouldn't poke his head out.

"I think he's sulking," said Alex. "Perhaps it's because the new patio has covered over his old favourite place?"

Alex and Hannah ran to tell Dad.

"I'm sure we can make him another patch," he reassured them. The children followed Dad into the garden and they all looked for a new patch for Sheldon.

"What about my bit of the garden?" asked Hannah.

Dad laughed. Everyone knew about Hannah's 'garden' and how she never, ever weeded it. It was a mass of wild strawberries, weeds and overgrown lettuces.

It was just the place for Sheldon!

Hannah picked him up and gently put him among the lettuces. She even brought out her dolls' house to take the place of the old shed. When Sheldon poked his head out of his shell he saw a gigantic lettuce towering above him. It looked delicious!

He was soon strolling happily around his new patch, inspecting the lettuces and nibbling on the wild strawberries. And, whilst he'd never admit it, Sheldon liked this new patch much more than the old one!

Cat Burglar

Tufty Tabby Cat was a greedy thief. When Tufty was around you daren't leave any food out, or he'd eat it up. Tufty's family knew this, and they always kept a close eye on him.

But not everyone in the street knew about Tufty's bad habits. When Mrs Topp at number 4 left a roast chicken by the open kitchen window, Tufty stole it clean away.

And no sooner had Dan Davey put down his pizza to open the front door, than Tufty had taken that too!

But Tufty was so clever that no one ever caught him.

One day as Tufty passed the block of flats, he lifted his nose and sniffed the air. He could smell tuna steak!

He looked up. And there it was – on a windowsill three floors up! But this wouldn't stop Tufty.

He clawed and scrambled his way onto a low roof, then up the drainpipe to the window ledge above.

With a purr of delight, Tufty gobbled up the tuna.

But, as you know, it is much easier to climb up than to climb down. And now Tufty was stuck up there.

Then he saw that the next-door window was open.

He easily jumped across and in through the window.

But there in the room was another cat – a big old grumpy tomcat.

"Go away!" hissed the cat, arching his back. But Tufty couldn't go anywhere. He was trapped!

Minutes later, the tomcat's owner came and found the two cats tumbling about the room in a hissing ball of fur and scratching claws.

She shooed poor Tufty Tabby Cat all the way down the stairs and out into the street, then threw a pan of water over him.

With his little heart thumping and soggy, wet fur, he limped home. Tufty had learned his lesson, and from then on he only ever ate from his *own* bowl!

Priscilla Pig

There was once a very ladylike pig called Priscilla. She thought she was the prettiest, cleanest pig in the whole world. And she probably was, as she was always washing herself in the pond.

But it wasn't always easy for Priscilla to *stay* clean, for she had to share her sty with twelve other very grubby pigs, and she often looked with a wrinkled-up snout at her mucky companions.

One day Farmer Stuart came into the sty with a man Priscilla hadn't seen before. The man pointed straight at Priscilla, who stood out amongst the muddy pigs.

"She looks like a fine pig," he said. "I'll have her."

"He chose me," boasted Priscilla to the other pigs after the man had gone. "And do you know why?"

"Because you're the pinkest, cleanest, most beautiful, and the most elegant pig in all the world!" chorused the other pigs, gently teasing Priscilla.

Then Sampson, the oldest and wisest pig, roared at Priscilla, "You foolish pig! You stood out too much. Don't you know what happens to pigs who leave the sty?"

"They go to a nice new home," Priscilla beamed.

"They're turned into sausages, that's what!" squeaked a cheeky little piglet. "Even I know that!"

Priscilla trembled. She hadn't thought of that. There was only one thing for it! Hardly believing what she was doing, she jumped into the mud and rolled and rolled in it until she was as mucky and grubby as the other pigs.

When the man returned he said, "I can't see that nice pink pig anywhere! But never mind, that one will do." And he picked up the cheeky young piglet.

"We'll have to clean him up, though. I don't want to put a dirty pig in a brand-new sty. The children at the farm park like to pet a nice clean pig!"

Poor Priscilla's heart sank. She'd missed out on a fine new home, but, to her surprise, she found she enjoyed rolling in the mud – well, just every now and again.

Silly Seth

Seth was a naughty monkey who loved to play tricks on the other animals. His favourite one was to hide in a tree and drop over-ripe fruit on their heads. *Splat!* Seth would laugh so hard he'd almost fall off the branch!

Most of the animals played along with Seth's tricks. Eddie the elephant would squirt the cheeky monkey with water, and Ryan the rhino would catch the squashy fruit on his horn.

But Zach the lion didn't think Seth's tricks were funny. After all, when you are the King of the Jungle, it's not very dignified to have rotten fruit dropped on you!

"When I catch you I'll eat you up!" Zach would roar. "You see if I don't!"

But Seth was far too quick to be caught, and he'd swing away through the treetops, giggling and shrieking.

But one day poor Seth was not so lucky.

He had just hit Zach – *splat!* – on the nose with a big squidgy mango and was about to race away through the treetops, when – *crack!* – the branch broke and Seth tumbled out of the tree right onto Zach's back!

"Grrraahhh!" snarled the lion. "Now I'll get you!"

Poor Seth dug his little hands into Zach's fur and hung on tightly. After all, Zach couldn't eat him if he was on the lion's back.

Zach shook himself hard and swished his tail, but
Seth didn't budge. The lion ran through the bushes and
across the plain, but Seth clung on, safely out of reach.

At last Zach reached a watering hole. Tired and hot,
he crouched down to lap thirstily. Very gently and very
quietly Seth slid off Zach's back, and went scampering
back to the jungle.

Zach gave a gigantic roar, but he didn't follow the little
monkey. He knew Seth wouldn't play his tricks again!

"Guy Will Get You!"

Guy was a huge gorilla who lived in a zoo. He was the most popular animal, but it wasn't because he was cute like the penguins or did tricks like the seals. Guy was everyone's favourite because he looked so ferocious!

"Watch out! Guy will get you!" the children would shout as they chased each other around the zoo.

But one day Guy did get out of his cage!

"Guy the gorilla is coming!" screamed the children. At first the zookeeper thought they were just playing one of their games.

The visitors ran to hide in the parrot house.

Guy sat down in the middle of the path. Where had all his human friends gone? He beat his chest and roared, just the way the visitors always liked.

One little girl called Daisy hadn't run away. She had visited Guy every weekend since she could remember. Daisy wasn't one tiny bit afraid of the gorilla. She could see that Guy just looked a little lonely.

Daisy went up to him and put her arms around his big, furry neck. Everyone in the parrot house gasped as Guy gave Daisy a very gentle hug back.

"Help! He's crushing my Daisy!" cried Daisy's mother.

"Don't be silly, Mum," said Daisy calmly. "Can't you see that he's a gentle gorilla, really?"

Arm in arm, Daisy led Guy back to his enclosure.

Slowly all the visitors came out from their hiding places. And by the time the zookeeper had arrived, a crowd had gathered around Guy, stroking his back and rubbing his head.

After that, more visitors than ever before came to see Guy. And Guy was very, very happy now his friends knew what a big softie he really was.

The Town Sheep

Layla Lamb was born in a farm park in the big city.

When she was tiny the children used to clamour to feed her from a baby's bottle and cuddle her. But now she was a fully-grown sheep they soon lost interest in her and went to see the ducklings or piglets instead.

One afternoon Mr Benson, who owned the farm, came to see her. "What will we do about you, Layla?" he sighed. "We've got two new lambs arriving tomorrow, and there's not enough room for you all."

Layla understood what Mr Benson meant. She knew that everyone would want to see the cute new lambs.

She would have to go. But what would happen to her? Mr Benson saw her worried expression.

"Do you know what, Layla," he smiled, "I've just had a splendid idea."

The very next day a small truck drew up at the farm park and Layla was led into the back of it.

She was driven for miles and miles until finally the truck stopped.

"Where on earth am I?" she wondered.

Layla lifted her head and sniffed the air.

It didn't smell like the city at all. She could smell fresh green grass and hay and flowers. Layla had arrived at a farm in the country.

You can imagine how different her new life was! She could roam freely on a green hillside with all the country sheep. They were all very friendly and made her feel welcome.

Every spring Layla was shorn and her thick coat spun into wool to make beautiful clothes.

Though she missed the children at the city farm, Layla knew that her real home was here in the country.

Lottie Lost

Emma looked everywhere, but her beloved little kitten, Lottie, was nowhere to be found. She had never run away before, and was always back in time for her dinner.

Mum looked worried. The little black and white cat always came when she banged her food bowl with a spoon, but no one had seen her since breakfast.

The very next day Mum and Dad put up notices all over the neighbourhood. But no one had seen Lottie anywhere.

That night Emma lay awake, wondering what had become of her kitten.

By the end of the week the family had begun to think that they might never see little Lottie again.

Then something rather strange happened.

Mrs Robinson over the road had been burgled on the day that Lottie disappeared. She told Emma's parents all about it.

"The police found the burglar lying sprawled in the gutter, surrounded by all the stolen goods!" explained Mrs Robinson. "They said he'd tripped over a cat that sprang out of the van when he opened the door."

A cat? When Emma heard the story she began to wonder. Could it have been Lottie?

But the burglar had been found fifty miles away and if the cat *had* been Lottie, she must now be well and truly lost. Emma hoped that Lottie would be safe so far from home, but she felt sure she would never see her again.

One evening, many weeks later, Mum was drawing the curtains. "Oh!" she suddenly cried. "Look who's in the garden!"

It was Lottie! She looked a lot thinner and her fur was dirty and scruffy, but she was alive and well.

With a cry Emma ran outside and gathered Lottie in her arms, hugging her tightly.

"Could she really have walked home that far?" wondered Emma.

She stroked Lottie's little pads, which looked muddy and worn.

"I think you really did," Emma sighed happily as Lottie nuzzled into her face, purring with happiness to be home again. "And you caught a burglar, too!"

Mrs Crabtree's Coat

Mrs Crabtree had a leopard-skin fur coat, of which she was very proud. But nowadays, hardly anyone wears fur coats. No one likes to think about animals being trapped for the sake of fashion.

But mean Mrs Crabtree didn't care.

If anyone asked her why she had a fur coat she would laugh in a horrible snorting sort of a way. "I'd rather have a dead leopard on my back than a live one!"

Every day Mrs Crabtree paraded up and down the street in her leopard-skin coat and matching hat, feeling very grand.

"If people like you stopped buying fur coats, no one would trap the poor animals any more," said Miss Dawson, her next-door neighbour.

But Mrs Crabtree paid no attention to her.

One afternoon Mrs Crabtree went to the zoo. Wearing her fur coat, her fur hat, a pair of leopard-skin gloves and a crocodile-skin handbag, she walked round the cages, pretending to admire the animals.

Not that she liked animals, of course. To Mrs Crabtree, visiting the zoo was like window-shopping. She only went to see which fur she would like next!

When she came to the leopard's enclosure it looked quite empty.

"Where are the leopards today?" she shouted rudely to the keeper.

"They're probably hiding," replied the keeper, glaring at Mrs Crabtree's fur coat disapprovingly.

Then Mrs Crabtree spotted a leopard staring at her with fierce green eyes from behind a tree.

Mrs Crabtree shivered.

But worse was to come. Suddenly Mrs Crabtree's coat began wriggling on her back! It made the most terrible snarling noises. And her hat was pawing at her hair and swishing its tail into her face!

"A tail? My hat doesn't have a tail," she thought, starting to panic.

Then the fur coat began clawing at her arms.

Terrified, Mrs Crabtree shut her eyes, and when she opened them she saw a real live leopard standing beside her, hungrily licking its lips!

Mrs Crabtree gave a terrified shriek and ran off down the path, coatless, hatless and gloveless.

She just remembered to throw the crocodile-skin handbag into the crocodile pool as she raced by. Otherwise, goodness knows what would have happened!

Strange to say, but no one else in the zoo saw the strange events. When she got to the zoo gates, Mrs Crabtree found no scratches on her arms, and the Head Zookeeper assured her that none of the leopards had escaped from their enclosure.

As soon as she got home, Mrs Crabtree packed up all of her fur coats and animal-skin handbags and put them away, and she hasn't even looked at a fur coat since that day at the zoo.

When Mrs Crabtree told her neighbour about her strange trip to the zoo, Miss Dawson remarked that perhaps it was her conscience that had come to life, not her coat at all.

Mrs Crabtree turned over a new leaf and she volunteered to work at the zoo to make amends for her bad ways. The Head Zookeeper set Mrs Crabtree on mucking out the elephant house straight away!

Unwise Owl

It was school report time and Oliver Owl was worried. He came from a family of very wise owls. But as Oliver's mum read his school report, it became very clear that he was not wise. Not clever. Not even smart.

"You're bottom of the class!" exclaimed his mum. "It says here that you can't add up and you can't spell!"

Mr Owl was even more upset. "We have a reputation to keep up, you know. We can't have an *unwise* owl!"

Feeling embarrassed, Oliver turned his head back to front, to hide from his parents.

The truth was, Oliver didn't see any point in learning to spell or add up. After all, all an owl was supposed to do was to catch mice. But Mr Owl never caught mice. Instead, he gave his wise advice to the other animals and birds in exchange for food for his family.

Oliver tried to explain, but his parents wouldn't listen and they sent him to bed early.

When Mr Owl woke up the next morning he had lost his voice. Mrs Owl made him honey tea to sooth his throat, but still his voice was just a tiny whisper.

All the animals who came for advice had to be been turned away. There was no food for the Owl family!

"Mum! Dad!" Oliver screeched excitedly. "I can help!"

"But how? You can't even spell 'mouse'!" said Mrs Owl, feeling very hungry.

Oliver didn't answer. He spread his wings and flew off silently over the wood. This was his chance to prove he was good at something!

By supper time Oliver had caught a dozen mice and he laid them proudly in front of his grateful parents.

"You've got a talent for hunting, son, and that's just as important as spelling and counting," wheezed Mr Owl. "If I were truly wise, I would have known that."

Jumping Jenna

Jumping Jenna was a kangaroo. She lived in a lovely zoo where she was very happy, but she wished that she had something special to do like the other animals.

The penguins put on a parade every day, which drew crowds of cheering visitors.

The camels gave children rides around the zoo, and even the seals had a balancing act that everyone loved.

But poor Jenna could only hoppity-hop around her enclosure, and she didn't think that was special enough.

One day Mr Jollyboat the zookeeper came to see Jenna. "The camels have all got colds and are tucked up in bed," he said. "And the rides are so popular. Nowadays people like theme parks and rollercoasters." Mr Jollyboat sighed. "If we can't give children rides, visitors will stop coming to the zoo."

"I can give the children rides!" offered Jenna.

"How?" asked Mr Jollyboat, astonished. "They would slide straight off your back!"

"You'll see!" said Jenna with a broad grin.

Soon a queue of small children was lined up waiting for a ride from Jenna – in her kangaroo's pouch!

It was terrific fun! Sometimes she jumped so high that it seemed to the children as if they were flying. It was even better than a rollercoaster!

In no time Jenna's rides became the most popular attraction at the zoo! And even the camels had to agree that her rides were the best.

Jenna jumped for joy.

Hayden Hare

One bright, early spring day Mrs Squirrel looked out of the window at her nice neat garden, only to see Hayden Hare running in circles, kicking up lumps of turf!

But before Mrs Squirrel could call out, Hayden leapt over the gate and was off down the lane.

There was a clatter and a crash and the sound of breaking glass. Hayden had crashed right into Mr Badger's milk float!

What a mess! There were broken bottles and white puddles of milk all over the road. But Hayden had already disappeared again.

"No milk today," said Mr Badger, looking at the mess.

"No lessons today," said Miss Goat, as she opened the door of Pepperpot School and saw the havoc Hayden Hare had caused there too.

The desks were tipped over. The blackboard was broken. And all the books were covered in paint.

But Hayden Hare still hadn't finished. He ran straight in front of the Reverend Tabbycat's bicycle, forcing him to swerve into the ditch.

Next, Hayden leapt into the village pond, scattering the ducks and frogs in all directions!

P.C. Collie caught up with Hayden just as the sun was setting and marched him off to the police station.

The next morning P.C. Collie let Hayden out of his cell. "You can go home now, Hayden."

Hayden looked confused. "But what am I doing here?"

Can you believe it? He couldn't remember a single thing about the chaos he had caused the day before.

"Something must have come over me," he said, when P.C. Collie told him what had happened.

"Of course! Yesterday was the first of March," said P.C. Collie. "It was the day for Mad March Hares!"

Hayden felt awful for all the trouble he'd made, so he went around the village helping to put everything right.

The School Pet

"Mum, please can we look after one of the school pets during the holidays?" asked Noah when he came home from school.

"I should think so," said his mum, thinking that a little hamster or rabbit would be rather fun.

"Thank you!" grinned Noah. And the next morning he gave his teacher the good news.

"Well," said his teacher. "Olivia is taking the guinea pigs. And Dylan is having the rabbit."

"Oh," said Noah.

"So that leaves Humphrey."

"Oh dear," said Noah. Humphrey was the school goat. "I hope Mum won't mind."

But when Noah's mum saw him leading a goat through the gate she nearly fainted. Especially as Humphrey was already tucking into her lovely roses.

"Noah!" she gasped. "What on earth is *that*?"

"It's Humphrey!" said Noah cheerfully. "He's the school pet we're looking after."

Humphrey burped as he munched on a tub of petunias. Noah's mum groaned. Why hadn't she asked what the school pet would be?

"Tie him to the apple tree for now," she said. "I'll have to think what to do with him."

Noah looped the rope around the apple tree in the garden. But no sooner had he turned his back, than Humphrey had chewed half the washing on the line.

"He's eaten my washing!" cried Mum. So Noah had to sit and watch Humphrey while Mum dashed out to the shop to look for some proper goat food.

"What do goats eat?" she wondered as she hurried out through the gate. "Apart from clothes and roses!"

"And Dad's onions!" Noah called after her, worriedly.

Noah's mum was gone for some time. When she finally returned she was followed by a small van.

"Noah!" she cried, sounding much more cheerful than when she had left. "I met the farmer's wife at the shops. She has come to take Humphrey to stay in their orchard. He can eat all the grass he likes, and there will be plenty of tasty windfall apples for him, too."

"Who's a lucky goat then?" said Noah, patting Humphrey happily. But Humphrey just burped.

An Unexpected Visitor

It was a sunny day, and the three bears decided to go for a walk to visit their friends on the other side of the forest. Now, this was the same bear family whose porridge had once been gobbled up by that naughty little girl, Goldilocks.

No sooner had the three bears disappeared into the shade of the trees, than someone crept out from behind the bushes by their house. He had golden curly hair – just like his older sister!

Goldilocks had often told her younger brother the story of her adventure. And so Curlylocks had wanted to see the three bears' house for himself and to try the three bowls of porridge, and sit in the three chairs, and sleep in the three beds!

Quick as a flash, he climbed up a tree and squeezed himself through an open window.

Oh dear! Curlylocks landed right on top of Baby Bear's rollerskates and went flying across the room.

He zoomed straight through the bedroom door and tumbled – *bump-bump-bump* – down the stairs, knocking Daddy Bear's best honeypot off its shelf.
Smash!

Dazed, Curlylocks staggered to his feet, but he tripped on the hall rug and banged into the kitchen table, where he fell face first into a cold bowl of porridge.

The naughty little boy wiped his face clean with the patchwork quilt that Mummy Bear had been sewing.

Just then the front door flew open.

"Who's broken my rollerskates?" wailed Baby Bear.

"Who's smashed my honeypot?" boomed Daddy Bear.

"And who's ruined my quilt?" shrieked Mummy Bear.

Curlylocks tried to hide, but it was no use.

The three bears marched Curlylocks all the way back to his home in the village. Curlylocks' dad was furious! First he made Curlylocks apologise. Then he promised the bears that his son would clean and tidy their house from top to bottom every week for a month. It was such a big job that he made Goldilocks help, too!

And ever since then, the three bears have never been bothered by those naughty children again!